I0628189

Wilfrid Scawen Blunt

Griselda

A Society Novel in Rhymed Verse

Wilfrid Scawen Blunt

Griselda
A Society Novel in Rhymed Verse

ISBN/EAN: 9783337030803

Printed in Europe, USA, Canada, Australia, Japan

Cover: Foto ©Andreas Hilbeck / pixelio.de

More available books at **www.hansebooks.com**

GRISELDA

A SOCIETY NOVEL IN RHYMED VERSE

" Unnatural? My dear, these things are life :
And life, some think, is worthy of the Muse."

LONDON
KEGAN PAUL, TRENCH, TRÜBNER, & CO. L^{TD}
PATERNOSTER HOUSE, CHARING CROSS ROAD
1893

GRISELDA

CHAPTER I.

AN idle story with an idle moral !

Why do I tell it, at the risk of quarrel

With nobler themes?   The world, alas ! is so,

And who would gather truth must bend him
   low,

Nor fear to soil his knees with graveyard ground,

If haply there some flower of truth be found.

For human nature is an earthy fruit,

Mired at the stem and fleshy at the root,

And thrives with folly's mixon best o'erlaid,

Nor less divinely so, when all is said.

Brave lives are lived, and worthy deeds are done

Each virtuous day, 'neath the all-pitying sun ;

5

But these are not the most, perhaps not even
The surest road to our soul's modern heaven.
The best of us are creatures of God's chance
(Call it His grace), which works deliverance ;
The rest mere pendulums 'twixt good and ill,
Like soldiers marking time while standing still.
'Tis all their strategy, who have lost faith
In things Divine beyond man's life and death,
Pleasure and pain.   Of heaven what know we,
Save as unfit for angels' company,
Say rather hell's ?   We cling to sins confessed,
And say our prayers still hoping for the best.
We fear old age and ugliness and pain,
And love our lives, nor look to live again.

I do but parable the crowd I know,
The human cattle grazing as they go,
Unheedful of the heavens.   Here and there
Some prouder, may be, or less hungry steer
Lifting his face an instant to the sky,
And left behind as the bent herd goes by,

Or stung to a short madness, tossing wild
His horns aloft, and charging the gay field,
Till the fence stops him, and he vanquished
    too,
Turns to his browsing—lost his Waterloo.

  The moral of my tale I leave to others
More bold, who point the finger at their brothers,
And surer know than I which way is best
To virtue's goal, where all of us find rest,
Whether in stern denial of things sweet,
Or yielding timely, lest life lose its feet
And fall the further.

          A plain tale is mine
Of naked fact, unconscious of design,
Told of the world in this last century
Of man's (not God's) disgrace, the XIXth.   We
Have made it all a little as it is
In our own images and likenesses,
And need the more forgiveness for our sin.

Therefore, my Muse, impatient to begin,
I bid thee fearless forward on thy road:
Steer thou thy honest course 'twixt bad and
    good.
Know this, in art that thing alone is evil
Which shuns the one plain word that shames the
    devil.
Tell truth without preamble or excuse,
And all shall be forgiven thee—all, my Muse !

.   .   .   .

In London then not many years ago
There lived a lady of high fashion, who
For her friends' sake, if any still there be
Who hold her virtues green in memory,
Shall not be further named in this true tale
Than as Griselda or the Lady L.,
Such, if I err not, was the second name
Her parents gave when to the font she came,
And such the initial letter bravely set
On her coach door, beneath the coronet,

Which bore her and her fortunes—bore, alas !
For, as in this sad world all things must pass,
However great and nobly framed and fair :
Griselda, too, is of the things that were.

But while she lived Griselda had no need
Of the world's pity.   She was proudly bred
And proudly nurtured.   Plenty her full horn
Had fairly emptied out when she was born,
And dowered her with all bounties.   She was
     fair
As only children of the noblest are,
And brave and strong and opulent of health,
Which made her take full pleasure of her wealth.
She had a pitying scorn of little souls
And little bodies, levying heavy tolls
On all the world which was less strong than
     she.
She used her natural strength most naturally,
And yet with due discretion, so that all
Stood equally in bondage to her thrall.

She was of that high godlike shape and size
Which has authority in all men's eyes:
Her hair was brown, her colour white and red,
Nor idly moved to blush.   She held her head
Straight with her back.   Her body, from the knee
Tall and clean shaped, like some well-nurtured
    tree,
Rose finely finished to the finger tips;
She had a noble carriage of the hips,
And that proportionate waist which only art
Dares to divine, harmonious part with part.
But of this more anon, or rather never.
All that the world could vaunt for its endeavour
Was the fair promise of her ankles set
Upon a pair of small high-instepped feet,
In whose behalf, though modestly, God wot.
As any nun, she raised her petticoat
One little inch more high than reason meet
Was for one crossing a well-besomed street.
This was the only tribute she allowed
To human folly and the envious crowd;

Nor for my part would I be found her judge
For her one weakness, nor appear to grudge
What in myself, as surely in the rest,
Bred strange sweet fancies such as feet suggest.
We owe her all too much. This point apart,
Griselda, modesty's own counterpart,
Moved in the sphere of folly like a star,
Aloof and bright and most particular.

By girlish choice and whim of her first will
She had espoused the amiable Lord L.,
A worthy nobleman, in high repute
For wealth and virtue, and her kin to boot ;
A silent man, well mannered and well dressed,
Courteous, deliberate, kind, sublimely blessed
With fortune's favours, but without pretence,
Whom manners almost made a man of sense.
In early life he had aspired to fame
In the world of letters by the stratagem
Of a new issue, from his private press,
Of classic bards in senatorial dress,

"*In usum Marchionis.*"   He had spent
Much of his youth upon the Continent,
Purchasing marbles, bronzes, pictures, gems,
In every town from Tiber unto Thames,
And gaining store of curious knowledge too
On divers subjects that the world least knew:
Knowledge uncatalogued, and overlaid
With   dust   and   lumber   somewhere   in   his
    head.

A slumberous man, in whom the lamp of life
Had never quite been lighted for the strife
And turmoil of the world, but flickered down
In an uncertain twilight of its own,
With an occasional flash, that only made
A deeper shadow for its world of shade.
When he returned to England, all admired
The taste of his collections, and inquired
To whose fair fortunate head the lot should fall
To wear these gems and jewels after all.
But   years   went   by,   and   still   unclaimed   they
    shone,

A snare and stumbling-block to more than one,
Till in his fiftieth year 'twas vaguely said,
Lord L. already had too long delayed.
Be it as it may, he abdicated life
The day he took Griselda to his wife.

And then Griselda loved him.   All agreed,
The world's chief sponsors for its social creed,
That, whether poor Lord L. was or was not
The very fool some said and idiot,
Or whether under cloak of dulness crass,
He veiled that sense best suited to his case,
Sparing his wit, as housewives spare their light,
For curtain eloquence and dead of night ;
And spite of whispered tales obscurely spread,
Doubting the fortunes of her nuptial bed,
Here at this word all sides agreed to rest :
Griselda did her duty with the best.

Yet, poor Griselda !   When in lusty youth
A love-sick boy I stood unformed, uncouth,

And watched with sad and ever jealous eye
The vision of your beauty passing by,
Why was it that that brow inviolate,
That virginal courage yet unscared by fate,
That look the immortal queen and huntress
    wore
To frightened shepherds' eyes in days of yore
Consoled me thus, and soothed unconsciously,
And stilled my jealous fears I knew not
    why?
How shall I tell the secret of your soul
Which then I blindly guessed, or how cajole
My boyhood's ancient folly to declare
Now in my wisdom the dear maid you were,
Though such the truth?

                  Griselda's early days
Of married life were not that fitful maze
Of tears and laughter which betoken aught,
Changed or exchanged, of pain with pleasure
    bought,

Of maiden freedom conquered and subdued,

Of hopes new born and fears of womanhood.

Those who then saw Griselda saw a child

Well pleased and happy, thoughtlessly beguiled

By every simplest pleasure of her age,

Gay as a bird just issued from its cage,

When every flower is sweet. No eye could
    trace

Doubt or disquiet written on her face,

Where none there was. And, if the truth be
    told,

Griselda grieved not that Lord L. was old.

She found it well that her sweet seventeen

Should live at peace with fifty, and was seen

Just as she felt, contented with her lot,

Pleased with what was and pleased with what was
    not.

She held her husband the more dear that he

Was kind within the bounds of courtesy,

And love was not as yet within her plan,

And life was fair, and wisdom led the van.

For she was wise—oh, wise ! She rose at eight
And played her scales till breakfast, and then sat
The morning through with staid and serious
    looks,
Counting the columns of her household books,
Her daily labour, or with puzzled head
Bent over languages alive and dead,
Wise as, alas ! in life those only are
Who have not yet beheld a twentieth year.
Wealth had its duties, time its proper use,
Youth and her marriage should be no excuse ;
Her education must be made complete !
Lord L. looked on and quite approved of it.
The afternoons, in sense of duty done,
Went by more idly than the rest had gone.
If in the country, which Lord L. preferred,
She had her horse, her dogs, her favourite bird,
Her own rose-garden, which she loved to rake,
Her fish to feed with bread crumbs in the lake,
Her schools, old women, poor and almshouses,
Her sick to visit, or her church to dress.

Lord L. was pleased to see her bountiful :
They hardly found the time to find it dull.

In London, where they spent their second year,
Came occupations suited to the sphere
In which they lived ; and to the just pretence
Of our Griselda's high-born consequence,
New duties to the world which no excuse
Admitted.   She was mistress of L. House
And heir to its traditions.   These must be
Observed by her in due solemnity.
Her natural taste, I think, repelled the noise,
The rush, and dust, and crush of London joys ;
But habit, which becomes a second sense,
Had reconciled her to its influence
Even in girlhood, and she long had known
That life in crowds may still be life alone,
While mere timidity and want of ease
She never ranked among youth's miseries.
She had her parents too, who made demand
Upon her thoughts and time, and close at hand

B

Sisters and friends. With these her days were
    spent
In simple joys and girlish merriment.
She would not own that being called a wife
Should make a difference in her daily life.

  Then London lacks not of attractions fit
For serious minds, and treasures infinite
Of art and science for ingenious eyes,
And learning for such wits as would be wise,
Lectures in classes, galleries, schools of art :
In each Griselda played conspicuous part—
Pupil and patron, ay, and patron-saint
To no few poor who live by pens and paint.
The world admired and flattered as a friend,
And only wondered what would be the end.

  And so the days went by. Griselda's face,
Calm in its outline of romantic grace,
Became a type even to the vulgar mind
Of all that beauty means when most refined,

The visible symbol of a soul within,

Conceived immaculate of human sin,

And only clothed in our humanity

That we may learn to praise and better be.

Where'er she went, instinctively the crowd

Made way before her, and ungrudging bowed

To one so fair as to a queen of earth,

Ruling by right of conquest and of birth.

And thus I first beheld her, standing calm

In the swayed crowd upon her husband's arm,

One opera night, the centre of all eyes,

So proud she seemed, so fair, so sweet, so wise.

Some one behind me whispered "Lady L. !

His Lordship too ! and thereby hangs a tale."

His Lordship ! I beheld a placid man,

With gentle deep-set eyes, and rather wan,

And rather withered, yet on whose smooth face

Time seemed to have been in doubt what lines to

trace

Of youth or age, and so had left it bare,

As it had left its colour to his hair.

An old young man perhaps, or really old,

Which of the two could never quite be told.

I judged him younger than his years gave right :

His looks betrayed him least by candlelight.

Yet, young or old, that night he seemed to me

Sublime, the priest of her divinity

At whose new shrine I worshipped.   But enough

Of me and my concerns !   More pertinent stuff

My tale requires than this first boyish love,

Which never found the hour its fate to prove.

My Lady smiling motions with her hand ;

The crowd falls back ; his Lordship, gravely
    bland,

Leads down the steps to where his footmen
    stay

In state.   Griselda's carriage stops the way !

And was Griselda happy?   Happy ?—Yes,

In her first year of marriage, and no less

Perhaps, too, in her second and her third.

For youth is proud, nor cares its last sad word

To ask of fate, and not unwilling clings

To what the present hour in triumph brings.

It was enough, as I have said, for her

That she was young and fortunate and fair.

The world that loved her was a lovely world,

The rest she knew not of.   Fate had not hurled

A single spear as yet against her life.

She would not argue as 'twixt maid and wife,

Where both were woman, human nature, man,

Which held the nobler place in the world's
    plan.

Her soul at least was single, and must be

Unmated still through its eternity.

And, even here in life, what reason yet

To doubt or question or despair of Fate?

Her youth, an ample web, before her shone

For hope to weave its subtlest fancies on,

If she had cared to dream.   Her lot was good

Beyond the common lot of womanhood,

And she would prove her fortune best in this,

That she would not repine at happiness.

Thus to her soul she argued as the Spring

Brought back its joy to each begotten thing—

Begotten and begetting. Who shall say

Which had the better reason, she or they?

In the fourth year a half acknowledged grief

Made its appearance in Griselda's life.

Her sisters married, younger both than she,

Mere children she had thought, and happily.

Each went her way engrossed by her new bliss,

Too gay to guess Griselda's dumb distress.

Her home was broken. In their pride they wrote

    wrote

Things that like swords against her bosom

    smote,

The detail of their hopes, and loves, and fears.

Griselda read, and scarce restrained her tears.

Her mother too, the latest fledgling flown,

Had vanished from the world. She was alone.

When she returned to London, earlier

Than was her custom, in the following year,

She found her home a desert, dark and gaunt ;

L. House looked emptier, gloomier than its
    wont.

Griselda sighed, for on the table lay

Two letters, which announced each in its way

The expected tidings of her sisters' joy.

Either was brought to bed—and with a boy.

Her generous heart leaped forth to these in
    vain,

It could not cheat a first sharp touch of pain,

But yielded to its sorrow.

                        That same night,

Lord L., whose sleep was neither vexed nor
    light,

And who for many years had ceased to dream,

Beheld a vision.   Slowly he became

Aware of a strange light which in his eyes

Shone to his vast discomfort and surprise ;

And, while perplexed with vague mistrusts and
    fears,
He saw a face, Griselda's face, in tears
Before him. She was standing by his bed
Holding a candle. It was cold, she said,
And shivered. And he saw her wrap her shawl
About her shoulders closely like a pall.
Why was she there ? Why weeping ? Why this
    light,
Burning so brightly in the dead of night ?
These riddles poor Lord L.'s half-wakened brain
Tried dimly to resolve, but tried in vain.

"I cannot sleep to-night," went on the voice,
"The streets disturb me strangely with their noise,
The cabs, the striking clocks." Lord L.'s dis-
    tress
Struggled with sleep. He thought he answered
    "Yes."
"What can I do to make me sleep ? I am ill,
Unnerv'd to-night. This house is like a well.

Do I disturb you here, and shall I go ?"

Lord L. was moved. He thought he answered
    " No."

" If you would speak, perhaps my tears would stop.
Speak ! only speak !"

                Lord L. here felt a drop

Upon his hand. She had put down the light,

And sat upon his bed forlornly white

And pale and trembling. Her dark hair unbound

Lay on her knees. Her lips moved, but their
    sound

Came strangely to his ears and half-unheard.

He only could remember the last word :

" I am unhappy—listen L. !—alone."

She touched his shoulder and he gave a groan.

" This is too much. You do not hear me. See,

I cannot stop these tears. Too much !"

                      And he

Now well awake, looked round him. He could
    catch

A gleam of light just vanished, and the latch

Seemed hardly silent.   This was all he knew.

He sat some moments doubting what to do,

Rose, went out, shivered, hearing nothing, crept

Back to his pillow, where the vision wept

Or seemed to weep awhile ago, and then

With some disquiet went to sleep again.

Next morning, thinking of his dream, Lord L.

Went down to breakfast in intent to tell

The story of his vision.   But he met

With little sympathy.   His wife was late,

And in a hurry for her school of art.

His lordship needed time to make a start

On any topic, and no time she gave.

Griselda had appointments she must save,

And could not stop to hear of rhyme or reason—

The dream must wait a more convenient season.

And so it was not told.

                              Alas, alas !

Who shall foretell what wars shall come to pass,

What woes be wrought, what fates accomplishèd,

What new dreams dreamt, what new tears vainly
    shed,
What doubts, what anguish, what remorse, what
    fears
Begotten in the womb of what new years !—
And all because of this, that poor Lord L.
Was slow of speech, or that he slept too well !

CHAPTER II.

THUS then it was.   Griselda's childhood ends

With this untoward night ; and what portends

May only now be guessed by those who read

Signs on the earth and wonders overhead.

I dare not prophesy.

                       What next appears

In the vain record of Griselda's years

Is hardly yet a token, for her life

Showed little outward sign of change or strife,

Though she was changed and though perhaps at

    war.

Her face still shone untroubled as a star

In the world's firmament, and still she moved,

A creature to be wondered at and loved.

Her zeal, her wit, her talents, her good sense
Were all unchanged, though each seemed more
    intense
And lit up with new passion and inspired
To active purpose, valiant and untired.
She faced the world, talked much and well, made
    friends,
Promoted divers schemes for divers ends,
Artistic, social, philanthropical :
She had a store of zeal for each and all.
She pensioned poets, nobly took in hand
An emigration plan to Newfoundland,
Which ended in disaster and a ball.
She visited St. George's hospital,
The Home for Fallen Women, founded schools
Of music taught on transcendental rules.
L. House was dull though splendid. She had
    schemes
Of a vast London palace on the Thames,
Which should combine all orders new and old
Of architectural taste a house could hold,

And educate the masses.   Then one day,
She fairly wearied and her soul gave way.

Again she sought Lord L., but not to ask
This time his counsel in the thankless task
She could no more make good, the task of living.
He was too mere a stranger to her grieving,
Her needs, her weakness.   All her woman's heart
Was in rebellion at the idle part
He played in her sad life, and needed not
Mere pity for a pain to madness wrought.
She did not ask his sympathy.   She said
Only that she was weary as the dead,
And needed change of air, and life, and scene :
She wished to go where all the world had been—
To Paris, Florence, Rome.   She could not die
And not have seen the Alps and Italy.
Lord L. had tried all Europe, and knew best
Where she could flee her troubles and find rest.
Such was her will.   Lord L., without more goad,
Prepared for travel—and they went abroad.

I will not follow here from day to day

Griselda's steps.   Suffice it if I say

She found her wished-for Paris wearisome,

Another London and without her home,

And so went on, as still the fashion was,

Some years ago, e'er Pulman cars with gas

And quick night flittings had submerged mankind

In one mad dream of luggage left behind,

By the Rhone boat to Provence.   This to her

Seemed a delicious land, strange, barren, fair,

An old-world wilderness of greys and browns,

Rocks, olive-gardens, grim dismantled towns,

Deep-streeted, desolate, yet dear to see,

Smelling of oil and of the Papacy.

Griselda first gave reins to her romance

In this forgotten corner of old France,

Feeding her soul on that ethereal food,

The manna of days spent in solitude.

Lord L. was silent.   She, as far away

Saw other worlds which were not of to-day,

With cardinals, popes, Petrarch and the Muse.

She stopped to weep with Laura at Vaucluse,

Where waiting in the Mistral poor Lord L.,

Who did not weep, sat, slept and caught a chill ;

This sent them southwards on through Christen-
    dom,

To Genoa, Florence, and at last to Rome,

Where they remained the winter.

                        Change had wrought

A cure already in Griselda's thought,

Or half a cure.   The world in truth is wide,

If we but pace it out from side to side,

And our worst miseries thus the smaller come.

Griselda was ashamed to grieve in Rome,

Among the buried griefs of centuries,

Her own sweet soul's too pitiful disease.

She found amid that dust of human hopes

An incantation for all horoscopes,

A better patience in that wreck of Time :

Her secret woes seemed chastened and sublime

There in the amphitheatre of woe.

She suffered with the martyrs. These would
  know,

Who offered their chaste lives and virgin blood,

How mortal frailty best might be subdued.

She saw the incense of her sorrow rise

With theirs as an accepted sacrifice

Before the face of the Eternal God

Of that Eternal City, and she trod

The very stones which seemed their griefs to sound

Beneath her steps, as consecrated ground.

In face of such a suffering hers must be

A drop, a tear in the unbounded sea

Which girds our lives. Rome was the home of
  grief,

Where all might bring their pain and find relief,

The temple of all sorrows : surely yet,

Sorrow's self here seemed swallowed up in it.

'Twas thus she comforted her soul. And then,

She had found a friend, a phœnix among men,

C

Which made it easier to compound with life,
Easier to be a woman and a wife.

   This was Prince Belgirate. He of all
The noble band to whose high fortune fall
The name and title proudest upon earth
While pride shall live by privilege of birth,
The name of Roman, shone conspicuous
The head and front of his illustrious house,
Which had produced two pontiffs and a saint
Before the world had heard of Charles le Quint ;
A most accomplished nobleman in truth,
And wise beyond the manner of his youth,
With wit and art and learning, and that sense
Of policy which still is most intense
Among the fertile brains of Italy,
A craft inherited from days gone by.
As scholar he was known the pupil apt
Of Mezzofanti, in whose learning lapped
And prized and tutored as a wondrous child,
He had sucked the milk of knowledge undefiled

While yet a boy, and brilliantly anon
Had pushed his reputation thus begun
Through half a score of tongues.   In art his place
Was as chief patron of the rising race,
Which dreamed new conquests on the glorious
    womb
Of ancient beauty laid asleep in Rome.
The glories of the past he fain would see
Wrought to new life in this new century,
By that continuous instinct of her sons,
Which had survived Goths, Vandals, Lombards,
    Huns,
To burst upon a wondering world again
With full effulgence in the Julian reign.

In politics, though prudently withdrawn
From the public service, which he held in scorn,
As being unworthy the deliberate zeal
Of one with head to think or heart to feel ;
And being neither priest, nor soldier, nor
Versed in the practice of Canonic lore,

He made his counsels felt and privately
Lent his best influence to " the Powers that be,"--
Counsels the better valued that he stood
Alone among the youth of stirring blood,
And bowed not to that Baal his proud knee,
The national false goddess, Italy.
He was too stubborn in his Roman pride
To trick out this young strumpet as a bride,
And held in classic scorn who would become
Less than a Roman citizen in Rome.
A man of heart besides and that light wit
Which leavens all, even pedantry's conceit.
None better knew than he the art to shew
A little less in talk than all he knew.
His manner too, and voice, and countenance,
Imposed on all, and these he knew to enhance
By certain freedoms and simplicities
Of language, which set all his world at ease.
A very peer and prince and paragon,
Griselda thought, Rome's latest, worthiest son,
An intellectual phœnix.

On her night

A sudden dawn had broke, portentous, bright.

Her soul had found its fellow.   From the day

Of their first meeting on the Appian Way,

Beside Metella's tomb, where they had discussed

The doubtful merit of a new found bust,

And had agreed to differ or agree,

I know not which, a hidden sympathy

Had taken root between them.   Either mind

Found in the other tokens of its kind

Which spoke in more than words, and naturally

Leaned to its fellow-mind as tree to tree.

Lord L., who had known the prince in other
          days,

While riding home had spoken in his praise,

And won Griselda's heart and patient smile,

For divers threadbare tales of blameless guile

Among the virtuosi, where the prince

Had played his part with skill and influence,

His sworn ally.   Lord L. grew eloquent,

Finding her ears such rapt attention lent,

And could have gone on talking all his life
About his friend's perfections to his wife.

Griselda listened.   In her heart there stirred
A strange unconscious pleasure at each word,
Which made the sunshine brighter and the sky
More blue, more tender in its sympathy.
The hills of the Campagna crowned with snow
Moved her and touched, she knew not why nor how.
The solemn beauty of the world; the fate
Of all things living, vast and inchoate
Yet clothed with flowers; the soul's eternal dream
Of something still beyond; the passionate whim
Of every noble mind for something good,
Which should assuage its hunger with new food;
The thrill of hope, the pulse of happiness,
The vague half-conscious longing of the eyes—
All these appealed to her, and seemed to lie
In form and substance under the blue sky,
Filling the shadows of the Sabine Hills
As with a presence, till her natural ills,

Transfigured through a happy mist of tears,
Gave place to hopes yet hardly dreamed as hers.
And still Lord L. talked calmly on, and she
Listened as to the voice of prophecy,
Nursing the pressure which the Prince's hand
Had left in hers, nor cared to understand.

From this day forth, I say, a tender mood
Possessed them both scarce conscious and un-
    wooed,
Even in the Prince, her elder and a man.
At least Griselda had no thought nor plan
Beyond the pleasure of a friendship dear
To all alike, Lord L., the Prince, and her :
No plan but that the day would be more sweet,
More full of meaning, if they chanced to meet ;
And this chanced every day. The Prince was
    kind
Beyond all kindness, and Lord L. could find
No words to speak his thanks he thus should be
The cicerone of their company.

And where a better ?   Belgirate's lore
In all things Roman was in truth a store
From which to steal.   At her Gamaliel's knees
Griselda sat and learned Rome's mysteries
With all the zeal of a disciple young
And strange to genius and a pleading tongue.
The Prince was eloquent.   His theme was high,
One which had taught less vigorous wings to fly,
The world of other days, the Pagan Rome,
The scarce less Pagan Rome of Christendom.
On these the Prince spoke warmly much and well,
Holding Griselda's patient ears in spell,
Yet broke off smiling when he met her eye
Fixed on his face in its mute sympathy :
A smile which was a question, an appeal,
And seemed to ask the meaning of her zeal.
He did not understand her quite.   He saw
Something beyond, unfixed by any law
Of woman's nature his experience knew :
He knew not what to hold or hope as true.
For she was young and sad and beautiful,

A very woman with a woman's soul.

She had so strange a pathos in her eyes,

A tone so deep, such echoes in her voice.

What was this Roman Hecuba to her?

This prate of consul, pontiff, emperor?

These broken symbols of forgotten pride?

These ashes of old fame by fame denied?

What were these stones to her that she should weep,

Or spend her passion on a cause less deep

Than her own joys and sorrows? Was it love,

Or what thing else had such a power to move?

If there was meaning in red lips! And yet

'Twere rank impiety to think of it.

An Italian woman—yes. But she? Who knew

What English virtue dared yet dared not do?

This was the thought which lent its mockery

To the more tender omen of his eye,

And checked the pride and chilled the vague
desire

Her beauty half had kindled into fire.

Yet hope was born and struggled to more life,

A puny infant with its fears at strife,

An unacknowledged hidden bastard child,

Too fair to crush, too wise to be beguiled ;

Even Griselda's prudery confessed

A star of Bethlehem risen in her East.

And thus the winter passed in happiness

If not in love.   I leave to each to guess

What name 'twere best to give it, for to some

Who judge such things by simple rule of thumb,

'Twill seem impossible they thus should meet

Day after day in palace, temple, street,

Beneath the sun of heaven or in the shade

Of those old gardens by the cypress made,

Or on their horses drinking in the wind

Of the Campagna, and with care behind,

Left to take vengeance upon poor Lord L.,

Some furlongs back a solemn sentinel,

Or in the twilight slowly stealing home

Towards the hundred cupolas of Rome,

To greet the new-born moon and so repeat
Old Tuscan ditties, tender, wise, and sweet,
To the light clatter of their horse-hoof's chime
In echoing answer of their terza-rhyme—
'Twill seem, I say, to some impossible
That all this was not love.   Yet, sooth to tell,
Easter had come and gone, and yet 'twas true
No word of love had passed between the two.

The fact is, after the first halcyon hour
When she had met the Prince and proved his power
To move her inmost soul, Griselda made
This compact with her heart no less than head,
Being a woman of much logic sense,
And knowing all, at least by inference :
She was resolved that, come what evil might
On her poor heart, the right should still be right,
And not a hair's-breadth would she swerve from this,
Though it should cost her soul its happiness.
She would not trifle longer, nor provide
The Prince with pretext for his further pride,

Or grant more favour than a friendship given
Once and for all, in this world as in heaven.
This she indeed could offer, but, if more
Were asked, why then, alas ! her dream was o'er.
I think no actual covenant had passed
In words between them either first or last,
But that the Prince, though puzzled and perplexed,
Had drawn a just conclusion from his text,
And read her meaning, while the hazard made,
Of certain idle words at random said,
Had sapped his confidence, and served to show
If speech were wise, 'twas wiser to forego.

Once too he wrote a sonnet. They had spent
An afternoon (it was in early Lent)
At that fair angle of the city wall
Which is the English place of burial,
A poet's pilgrimage to Shelley's tomb,—
The holiest spot, Griselda thought, in Rome,—
A place to worship in, perhaps to pray,
At least to meditate and spend the day.

She had brought her friend with her.   She had
    at heart
To win his homage for the unknown art
Of this dead alien priest of Italy,
This lover of the earth, and sea, and sky ;
And, reading there and talking in that mood
Which comes of happiness and youthful blood
So near akin to sorrow, their discourse
Had touched on human change and pain's remorse
Amid the eternal greenness of the spring ;
And, when they came to part, there had seemed
    to ring
A note of trouble in Griselda's voice,
A sigh as if in grief for human joys,
An echo of unspoken tenderness,
Which caused the Prince to hold her hand in his
One little moment longer than was right,
When they had shaken hands and bid good night.

And so he wrote that evening on the spur
Of the first tender impulse of the hour

A sonnet to Griselda, a farewell
It seemed to be, yet also an appeal—
Perhaps a declaration ; who shall say
Whether the thought which lightened into day,
Between the sorrowing accents of each line,
Was more despair or hope which asked a sign ?

" Farewell," it said, " although nor seas divide
Nor kingdoms separate, but a single street,
The sole sad gap between us, scarce too wide
For hands to cross, and though we needs must
    meet
Not in a year, a month, but just to-morrow,
When the first happy instinct of our feet
Bears us together,—yet we part in sorrow,
Bidding good-bye, as though we would repeat
Good-byes for ever.   There are gulfs that yawn
Between us wide with time and circumstance,
Deep as the gulf which lies 'twixt dead and dead.
The day of promise finds no second dawn :
See, while I speak, the pressure of our hands

Fades slowly from remembrance, and is fled,

And our weak hearts accept their fate.   Nay, nay,

We meet again, but never as to-day."

To this Griselda answered nothing.   She

Was pleased, yet disconcerted.   Poetry

Is always pleasant to a woman's ear,

And to Griselda had been doubly dear,

If it had touched less nearly.   But her heart

Had bounded with too violent a start

To leave her certain of her self-control,

In this new joy which seemed to probe her

   soul.

And feeling frightened she had tried to find

A reason for the tumult of her mind

In being angry.   He should not have dared

To strike so near the truth.   Or had she bared

Her soul so plain to his that he should speak

Of both as an eye-witness?   She felt weak

And out of temper with herself and him,

And with the sudden waking from a dream

Too long indulged, and with her own sad fate,
Which made all dreams a crime against the State.
There yawned indeed a gulf between them.
    This
It needed no such word as had been his
To bring back to her memory or show
How wide it was, and deep, and far below ;
And yet she shuddered, for already thought
Had led her to the brink where reason fought
With folly, and conjured it to look down
Into the vast and terrible unknown.
This was itself an omen.

               All that day
Griselda had a headache, and said nay
To those who called, the Prince among the rest,
Who came distrusting and returned distressed.
Awhile this humour lasted. Then they met,
And Belgirate, venturing a regret
For having vexed her with so poor a rhyme,
Griselda had protested want of time

And want of talent as her sole excuse

For having made no answer to his Muse,

Yet cast withal a look so pitiful

Upon his face it moved his very soul.

This closed the incident.   He might have spoken

Perhaps that instant, and received some token

Of more than a forgiveness.   But his fate

Had willed it otherwise or willed too late.

For love forgives not, plead it as we may

To speak the unspoken " Yes " of yesterday.

D

CHAPTER III.

Who has not seen the falls of Tivoli,
The rocks, the foam-white water, and the three
Fair ruined temples which adorn the hill?
Who has not sat and listened to the shrill
Sweet melody of blackbirds, and the roar
Of Anio's voice rebounding from the shore,
Nor would have given his very soul to greet
Some passing vision of a white nymph's feet,
And weaving arms, as the wild chasm's spray
Beat on his face, for ever answering "Nay?"
Who has not turned away with sadder face,
Abashed before the genius of the place,
A wiser man, and owned upon his knees,
The dull transmontane Goth and boor he is?
Who that was born to feel?

What sons of clay

Are these that stand among your shrines to-day,

Gods of the ancient rivers ! and who set

The heavy impress of barbarian feet

Upon your classic shores, and dare to love

Your ruined homes in temple, rock, and grove !

What new rude sons of Japhet !   What mad
    crew,

Whose only creed is what it dares to do

Through lack of knowledge, whose undoubting
    heart,

Here in the very temples of old art,

Brings out its little tribute, builds its shrines,

Wreathes its sad garlands of untutored lines,

Writes, paints, professes, sculptures its new gods,

And dares to have its home in your abodes !

Oh, if I had a soul oppressed with song,

A tongue on fire to prophesy among

My brother prophets, if I had a hand

Which needs must write its legend on life's sand

With brush or chisel, I at least would choose
Some soil less fair, less sacred to the Muse,
Some younger, wilder land, where no sad voice
Had ever stammered forth its tale of joys,
And loves and sorrows, or in tones less rude
Than the brute pulsing of its human blood ;
If I would build a temple, it should be
At least not here, not here in Italy,
Where all these temples stand.   My thought
    should shape
Its fancies in rough granite on some cape
O'erlooking the Atlantic, from whose foam
No goddess ever leaped, and not in Rome,
Beneath the mockery of immortal eyes,
Gazing in marble down, so coldly wise !

  Such   was   Griselda's   thought,   which,   half
    aloud,
She uttered one May morning 'mid a crowd
Of pleasure-seekers, come from Rome to see
The wonder of these falls of Tivoli,

And Belgirate's villa, where the Prince
Was offering entertainment (for his sins),
And dancing to all such as called him friend
That Spring in Rome, now nearly at an end ;—
A thought suggested by the place and by
A German painter, who undauntedly
Was plying a huge canvas just begun,
With brush and palette seated in the sun.
She had hardly meant to speak, and when Lord I.
Objected (for he knew his classics well)
That landscape-painting was an unknown trade
In the days of Horace, blushed for her tirade,
And turned to Belgirate, who stood near,
Playing the host to all the world and her.

    The Prince appealed to, though his care was less
With what was spoken than the speaker's face,
Took up the parable, confessed the truth
Of all each ventured, and agreed with both.
Nature, he said, and art, though now allied,
Had not in all times thus walked side by side.

Indeed the love of Nature, now so real,

Was alien to the love of the ideal,

The classic love which claimed as though of need

Some living presence for each fountain-head,

Each grove, each cavern, satyr, nymph, or god,

A human shape unseen yet understood.

This was the thought which lived in ancient art,

Eschewing the waste places of the heart,

And only on compulsion brought to face

Brute Nature's aspect in its nakedness.

Nature as Nature was a thought too rude

For these, untempered in its solitude.

It had no counterpart in our new love

Of mountain, sea and forest.   Then, each grove

Asked for its statue, each perennial spring

Its fountain.   Solitude itself must bring

Its echo.   Every mountain top of Greece

Beheld fair temples rise.   A law of peace

Reigned over art in protest at the mood

Of social life which drenched the world in blood.

All now had been reversed.   Our modern creed

Scouted the law that men were born to bleed.

It turned from human nature, if untaught,

And wrought mankind, perhaps and overwrought

Into trim shapes, and then for its relief

Rushed to the wilderness to vent its grief

In lonely. passion.   Here it neither sought

Nor found a presence which it needed not.

It chose wild hills and barren seas.   It saw

Beauty in tumult, in revolt a law.

Here it gave reins to its brute instincts.   Here

It owned no god, no guide, no arbiter.

Its soul it must avenge of discipline,

And Nature had gone naked from the shrine.

This was its consolation.

                    Of the score

Who stood around him and who praised his lore,

Perhaps no single listener understood

The thought which underlay the Prince's mood,

Or guessed its bitterness—not even she

Who lent the moral to his mockery.

Yet she was moved.   In her too was a need
Of consolation for too fair a creed,
An impulse of rebellion.   In her blood
There lived a germ of Nature unsubdued,
Which would not be appeased. She too had sought
A refuge from the tyranny of thought
In the brute impulses of sea and plain
And cloud and forest far from haunts of men.
A vain mad search.   The fetters of her pride
Galled her like sores. Griselda turned and sighed.

That evening on the terrace, vaguely lit
With paper lanterns and the infinite
Display of those fair natural lamps, the stars,
And 'neath the influence of the planet Mars
Or Venus or another—which it was
We best may judge by that which came to pass—
The Prince essayed his fortune.

                              From the hour
Of their first flash of eloquence, some power,

Some most persistent and ingenious fate
Of idle tongues had held them separate,
Griselda and the Prince—him in his part
Of host, with cares not wholly of the heart
Demanding his attention, while on her
Friends fastened more than dull and less than dear.
In vain they stopped, and loitered, and went on,
Leaving no trick untried, unturned no stone ;
In vain they waited. Still their hope deferred
Failed of its object, one consoling word,
One little sigh as of relief thus given :
"Well, they are gone at last, and thanked be
    Heaven."
But hour on hour went by, and accident
Seemed still at pains to frustrate their intent,
Piling up grief for them and poor Lord L.,
On whom, in fault of foes, their vengeance fell.
'Twas worst for her. She knew not whom to strike,
Lord L., her friends, the Prince—'twas now alike.
She had lost in fact her temper, if I dare
Thus speak of one so wise and one so fair,

And to the point that now there was no room
For other thought, but L. should take her home,
Away and speedily.

                    The Prince, who knew
No word of what a storm Fate held in brew,
And who had sought, in innocence of all,
Griselda's hand to lead the opening ball,
And sought in vain, now found, to his despair,
My lady cloaked and standing on the stair.
She was alone.   "Lord L. had gone," she said,
"To bid the Prince good night.   Her foolish head
Had played her false, and ached with the new heat
Of the May sun (even L. complained of it).
They must be home betimes.   Next day was
          Sunday,
And they had much to do 'twixt that and Monday,
In view of their departure."   "Whither? whence?
In Heaven's name," exclaimed the astounded Prince.
"Why, home to England, she had thought he
          knew:

She must have told him.   L. was more than due

In London, where his place in Parliament

Required his presence.   He had missed the Lent,

And dared not miss the Easter session.   She

Thought he was right, altho',"—and suddenly

She burst in tears.   The Prince, in dire distress,

Besought her to be calm.   But she, with face

Hid in both hands, and turning from the light,

Broke from his arms, and rushed into the night.

Across the hall, beneath the portico,

And down the steps she fled, to where below

The garden lay all dim with starlit shade,

And the white glimmer of the main façade.

Here Belgirate found her on a seat,

Crouched in an angle of the parapet,

And sobbing as in terror.   His surprise

Was changed to resolution.   To his eyes

The world became transfigured.   "Lady L.,"

He whispered, "what is this?   You love me?   Well,

Why do you weep?"

　　　　　　　He took her hands in his
And pressed them to his lips ; and at the kiss
Griselda started from the heap she was
And sat upright, with pale pathetic face
Turned to the night.　By the dim starlight he
Beheld, half-awed and half in ecstasy,
The strange emotion of her countenance.
She made no gesture to withdraw her hands,
No sign of disagreement with his words.
Her eyes looked scared and troubled like a bird's
Caught in a net, and seemed to ask of Fate
Where the next blow should fall.　'Twas thus she
　　　sat
Speechless, inanimate, nor seemed to breathe.
The Prince could hear the chattering of her teeth,
And feel her shiver in the warm night wind,—
And yet its touch was hardly thus unkind.

　　He too, poor soul, in hope and tenderness,
　　Still kissed her hands, and kissed her gloves and
　　　dress,

And kneeling at her feet embraced her knees
With soothing arms and soft cajoleries.
She dared not turn nor speak.   The balustrade
Served as a pretext for her with its shade
Hiding his face.   She would not seem to guess
All that his fondness asked of her distress :
A word might break the spell.   She only knew
She was a poor sad woman, doomed to do
Sorrow to all who loved her, that the Prince
Had spoken truly, and her long pretence
Of innocence was o'er.   She scorned to make
An idle protest now for honour's sake.
He had a right to ask for what he would
Now that she loved him, and her womanhood
Reserved one tearful right, and only one,
To hide her face an instant and be gone.

How long they sat thus silent who shall say ?
Griselda knew not.   Time was far away ;
She wanted courage to prepare her heart
For that last bitterest word of all, "We part ; "

And he cared naught for time : his heaven was
    there,
Nor needed thought, nor speech, nor even prayer.

A sound of music roused them. From the house
Voices broke in and strains tumultuous,
Proving the dance begun. Then with a sigh
Griselda turned her head, and piteously
Looked in his face. She moved as if to go,
And when he held her still, " For pity, no,
Let me be gone," she cried. " I ask it thus,"
Clasping her hands. "You will not? No ! alas !
You must not doubt me when I speak the truth :
This is a great misfortune for us both."
" Griselda," he began. "Oh, stop," she said,
"You know not what you ask." She bent her
    head
Close to his own. "I am not what I seem,
A woman to be loved, not even by him
Whom I might choose to worship. Mine must be
An unfinished life, not quite a tragedy,

Even to my friends, an idle aimless life,

Not worth an argument, still less a strife.

You must forget, forgive me.   We were friends,

Friends still perhaps; but, oh! this first day
    ends

Our love for ever.   What you said was true,

Only I never guessed it."

                         The Prince knew

That she was weeping, and a single sob

Broke from her lips.   She seemed her wounds to
    probe.

"Yes, I have loved you, loved you from the
    first,

The day we met at Terni, when you burst

Like sunshine on the storm of my dark life—

You, wise and free—I, only the sad wife

Of one you called a friend.   The fault was mine

And mine alone.   In you there was no sin :

You stood too far from me, too high above

My woman's follies even to dream of love.

There, do not answer. You were kind to me,
Good, patient, wise—you could no other be—
But, oh ! you never loved me."

                                        Here again
The Prince broke in protesting (but in vain) :
Her words were madness and his heart was hers.
She would not listen nor control her tears—
"You never loved me. This one thought I hold
In consolation of my manifold
Deceits and errors. You at least are free
From all deceptions and remorse and me :—
I cannot cause you sorrow, else it were
Indeed too pitiful, too hard to bear."

She stooped and kissed his forehead reverently,
As one would kiss a relic ; and when he
Still would have spoken, stopped him with a hand
Laid on his lips, half-prayer and half-command.
She would not let him speak. The prince, tho' mute,
Now pleaded with his hands and pressed his suit

With better eloquence, for this to her

Seemed less a crime than speech.   Her ignorant fear

Had hardly fathomed yet the troubled sea

On which her lot was cast thus dangerously.

She only feared his words to prove him right ;

And these caresses in the dim still night

Soothed and consoled her.   They were too unreal,

Too strange to her experience, quite to feel

Or quite to question.   She, with half-shut eyes,

And face averted, ceased to feel surprise,

And ceased to think.   She was a child again,

Caressed and fondled.   She forgot her pain,

And almost even his presence in the place.

He was too near and could not see her face.

Besides, Griselda loved him.   Only once

She made a silent protest with her hands,

As one might make asleep, and in her dream

Opened her eyes, and seemed to question him

With the pathetic instinct as of doom.

The Prince in rapture judged his hour was come.

E

Alas ! poor Prince.   If thou hadst had thy bliss,

I would not then have grudged thy happiness,

Thine nor Griselda's.   Happiness is not

A merchandise men buy or leave unbought

And find again.   It is a wild bird winging

Its way through heaven, in joyous circles ringing,

Aloft, at its own will.   Then, e'er we wist,

It stooped and sat a moment on our wrist,

And fondled with our fingers, and made play

With jess and hood as if it meant to stay.

And we, if we were wise and fortunate,

And if the hour had been decreed of fate,

Seized the glad bird and held it in our hand,

And forced it to obey our least command,

Knowing that never more, if not made sure,

It would come again to voice, or sign, or lure.

Oh, such is happiness.   That night for them

Fate stood, a genius, suppliant and tame,

Demanding to do service.   Had they willed,

The treasure-house of heaven had been unfilled

And emptied in their lap.   They too, even they,

Mere mortals born, inheritors of clay,

Had known eternal life, and been as gods,

Only the will between them was at odds,

Only the word was wanting.

What one thing

It was that frightened Fate to taking wing,

And scared for ever the celestial bird,

And left them desolate, if I have heard

I do not now remember, nor would say

Even if I knew.   'Twas told me not to-day

Nor yesterday, but in a time long since,

By one of the two who knew, in confidence,

And then not quite perhaps the utter truth—

Whoever tells it?   But there came to both

A moment when, as Belgirate knew,

There was no further power to plead or sue :

They had played with Fate too long.   Their hour
    was over ;

She was no more his love nor he her lover.

His courage was exhausted.   One by one
His fingers, which still held Griselda's gown,
Relaxed their hold.   His hands dropped by his side,
His head upon his bosom, and the pride,
Which was the reason of his being, quailed.
Grief in that hour and tenderness prevailed,
And tears rushed to his eyes, long strangers there,
And to his lips, Italian-like, a prayer,
While he lay prostrate, his face turned from heaven,
Under the stars.

        The tower clock struck eleven
And roused him.   He had neither heard nor known
Griselda's going, but he was alone.

.   .   .   .

And she?   Griselda?   In a whirl of grief,
Tortured, distracted, hopeless of relief,
And careless now what eye should see her tears,
Whom none could mock with bitterer jibes than
    hers,

And speechless to all question of her lord,
Who sought to learn what portent had occurred,
And still reverted to the theme begun
Of Roman fever and the Roman sun ;
She was driven back to Rome.   Two days her door
Was shut to all the world, both rich and poor,
And on the third she went to Ostia,
Pleading a wild desire to see the sea.

The sea !   What virtue is there in the sea
That it consoles us thus in misery ?
In joy we do not love it, and our bliss
Scoffs at its tears and scorns its barrenness.
Our pride of life is in the fruitful Earth,
The mother of all joy, which gave us birth,
The Earth so touching in its hopes to be,
So green, so tender in its sympathy.
But when life turns to bitterness—ah ! then,
Where is Earth's message to the sons of men ?
How does she speak ?   What sound of grief is hers
To match our grief ?   What tale of pity stirs

Her jubilant heart ? The laughing woods give back
Naught of their happiness to those who lack.
The beauty of the uplands bars relief,
The prosperous fields are insolent to grief ;
There is no comfort in the lowing herds,
The hum of bees, the songs, the shouts of birds ;
There is no sob in all the living earth,
Naught but the flutter of discordant mirth,
On which, as on a pageant, morn and even
The careless sun shines mockingly from heaven.
There is no grief in all the world save one,
The ocean's voice, as tearful as our own.
Then from the Earth we turn—too potent mother,
Too joyous in her offspring—to that other,
The childless, joyless, unproductive Sea,
And mourn with her her dread virginity.
We clasp her naked rocks with our two hands,
Barefoot we tread her barren waste of sands,
Her breadths of shingle and her treeless shore,
Knowing her griefs are as our griefs, and more,
An eternal lack of love.

'Twas in this guise
Griselda cradled her soul's miseries,
And nursed it in its anguish like a child,
And soothed it to oblivion.   The sea smiled
With its eternal smile upon her sorrow,
The selfsame yesterday, to-day, to-morrow,
And kept its tears in its own bosom sealed,
A mystery of passion unrevealed,
Save in the tremor of its voice at noon,
When the wind rose and played wild chords thereon.
So she.

The memory of that place long stood
In her remembrance as a dream of good,
Dividing life as sleep divides the day,
A place of utter weakness.   Let those say
Who will, that deeds of strength life's milestones
    are.
The dearest days are not the days of war,
And victory is forgotten in the peace
Of certain hours gone by in helplessness,

When the soul ceased to battle, and lay still
As on a deathbed dumb to good and ill.
These are its treasures.

Nor was silence all
Griselda's ointment.   Hard by the sea-wall,
Where daily her steps turned fresh peace to find,
A convent stood, inviting to the mind.
Here she found entrance at the chapel gate,
And knelt in prayer half-inarticulate,
Bowed to the earth.   For patron saints it had
The Marys three — "two virtuous, and one
      bad,"
Griselda thought, "like her own self"—who came
In flight together from Jerusalem,
And landed there ; and these in her great need,
She suppliant asked for her soul's daily bread,
Using all fondest words her lips could frame,
To speak her secret wishes without blame.
Six candlesticks she vowed, to each a pair,
So they would listen to and grant her prayer.

The superstition pleased her.   In her pride
She bowed and begged like any peasant's bride,
For what? for whom? she hardly could explain
Even to her, the dear St. Magdalen.
"And yet," she argued, "she at least will know
And understand me if no other do."

All this was folly, but it comforted
And gave her strength.   Then with a calmer head,
If not a calmer heart, she turned once more
From love to life.   Her first strong grief was o'er.

CHAPTER IV.

How shall I take up this vain parable
And ravel out its issue? Heaven and hell,
The principles of good and evil thought,
Embodied in our lives, have blindly fought
Too long for empire in my soul to leave
Much for its utterance, much that it can grieve.
A soldier on the battlefield of life,
I have grown callous to the signs of strife,
And feel the wounds of others and my own
With scarce a tremor and without a groan.
I have seen many perish in their sins,
Known much of frailty and inconsequence,
And if I laughed once, now I dare not be
Other than sad at man's insanity.
Therefore, in all humility of years,

Colder and wiser for hopes drowned in tears,
And seeking no more quarries for my mirth,
Who most need pity of the sons of earth,
I dip in kindlier ink my chastened pen,
And fill of my lost tale what leaves remain.

Years passed. Griselda from my wandering
   sight
Had waned and vanished, like a meteor bright,
Leaving no pathway in my manhood's heaven,
Save only memories vaguely unforgiven
Of something fair and sad, which for a day
Had lit its zenith and had gone its way.
Rome and the Prince, the tale that I had heard,
Griselda's beauty—all that once had stirred
My curious thought to wonder and regret,
In the vexed problem of her woman's fate,
Had yielded place to the world's work-day cares,
The wealth it covets and the toil it dares.
I was no more a boy, when idle chance
And that light favour which attends romance

Brought me once more within the transient spell

Of other days, and dreams of Lady L.

'Twas in September (I have always found

That month in my life's record dangerous ground,

Whether it be due to some unreasoned stress

Of the mad stars which dog our happiness,

Or whether—since in truth most things are due

To natural causes, if our blindness knew—

To the strong law of Nature's first decay,

Warning betimes of time that cannot stay,

And summer perishing, and hours to come,

Lit by less hope in the year's martyrdom ;

And so we needs must seize at any cost

Fleet pleasure's hem lest all our day be lost)

'Twas in September, at a country house

In the Midland shires, where I had come, God

knows,

Without a thought but of such joyous sort

As manhood ventures in the realms of sport

With that dear god of slaughter England's sons

Adore with incense-smoke and roar of guns,

That this new chapter opens. Who had guessed

So rare a phœnix housed in such a nest?

  For we, in truth, were no wise company,

Men strong and joyous, keen of hand and eye,

And shrewd for pleasure, but whose subtlest wit

Was still to jest at life while using it,

And jest at love, as at a fruit low hung

To all men's lips, no matter whence it sprung.

A fool's philosophy, yet dear to youth

Bred without knowledge of the nobler truth,

And seeming wisdom, till the bitter taste

Of grief has come to cure its overhaste.

Naught was there, in the scene nor in the parts

Played by the actors, worthy serious hearts,

Or worthy her whose passion trod a stage

High o'er the frailties of our prurient age,

Griselda and her unattained fair dream

Of noble deeds and griefs unknown to them.

How came she there?

               Our hostess was a woman
Less famed for wisdom than a heart all human,
Rich in life's gifts, a wealthy generous soul,
But still too fair and still too bountiful.
The rest, mad hoydens of the world, whose worth
Lay mired with folly, earthiest of the earth.
How came she there?

               When I, unconscious all
Of such high presence at our festival,
Heard her name bandied in the general hum
Of hungry tongues, which told the guests had
    come,
And saw in converse with our host the form,
Familiar once in sunshine and in storm,
Of her who was to me the type and sign
Of all things noble, not to say Divine,
Breathing the atmosphere of that vain house,
My heart stopped beating.   Half incredulous,
I looked and questioned in my neighbours' eyes,
Seeking the sense of this supreme surprise.

My thought took words, as at the table set

Men's lips were loosed, discoursing while they
    ate,

And each to each.

                                    Beside me, of the crew

Of gilded youths who swelled the retinue

Of our fair hostess in her daily lot

Of hunting laughter when field sports were not,

Sat one, a joyous boy, whom fashion's freak,

A mad-cap courage and a beardless cheek,

Had set pre-eminent in pleasure's school

To play the hero and to play the fool

For those few years which are the summer's day

Of fashion's foils ere they are cast away.

Young Jerry Manton !   Happy fortune's son,

What heights of vanity your creed had won,

Creed of adventure, and untiring words

And songs and loves as brainless as a bird's.

Who would not envy you your lack of sense,

Your lawless jibes, your wealth of insolence,

The glory of your triumphs unconcealed
In pleasure's inmost and most sacred field !
Who would not share the sunshine of your mirth,
Your god-like smile, your consciousness of worth,
The keenness of your wit in the world's ways,
Your heart so callous to its blame or praise!
Him I addressed, in pursuance of my doubt
How such a prodigy had come about.

Young Manton eyed me. " Every road," he said,
"Leads—well—to Rome."   He laughed and
        shook his head,
As if in censure of a thought less sage.
" My lady's thirty is a dangerous age,
And of the three where most misfortunes come
Is the worst strewn with wrecks in Christendom."
" You see," he added, "we are not all wise
In all dilemmas and all companies,
And there are times and seasons when the best
Has need of an hour's frolic with the rest,
If only to set free the importunate load

Of trouble pressing on an uphill road.

Women's first snare is vanity.   At twenty

Praises are pleasant, be they ne'er so plenty ;

And some, the foolish ones, are thus soon caught

Seeking to justify the flattery taught.

These are the spendthifts, dear ingenuous souls,

Whose names emblazoned stand on pleasure's rolls,

Manning the hosts of mirth.   Apart from them,

More serious or less eager in their aim,

The wise ones wait like birds that hold aloof,

Conscious of danger and the cloven hoof.

Yet there are times."

He paused awhile and sighed.

" The second snare," said he, " is set less wide ;

It stands midway between the dawn of youth

And beauty's sunset, with its naked truth,

A danger hidden cunningly in flowers,

And the wild drowsing of the noontide hours.

Here fall the elect, the chosen virtuous few,

Who have outlived the worst the storm could do,

F

But faint when it is over, through mere stress
Of their mortality's first weariness.
'Tis hard to see youth perish, even when
Ourselves to the mad warrant have set pen ;
And for the wisest there are days of grief
And secret doubts and hours of unbelief
In all things but the one forbidden bliss
Churchmen forbid, and poets call a kiss.
Why should we wonder ?   'Tis a kindlier fate
At least than that, the last, which comes too late,
The old fool's folly nursed at forty-five.
Griselda is an angel, but alive,
Believe me, to her wings."   A fatuous flush
Mantled his face, not quite perhaps a blush,
But something conscious, as of one who knows.
" Virtue and pleasure are not always foes,"
He sighed.   "And much depends upon the man."

    I turned impatient.   There, behind her fan,
At the far table's end, Griselda's eyes
Were watching us, half hid by its disguise,

But conscious too, as if a secret string
Had vibrated 'twixt her and that vain thing,
The cynic boy, whose word was in my ear,
Dishonouring to me and him and her.
Our eyes met, and hers fell ; a sudden pain
Touched me of memory, and in every vein
Ran jealous anger at young Manton's wit,
While, half aloud, I flung my curse on it.

Later, I found Griselda gravely gay,
And glad to see me in the accustomed way
Of half affection my long zeal had won,
Her face no older, though the years had spun
Some threads unnoticed in her fair brown hair
Of lighter hue than I remembered there,
Less silver streaked than gold. All else had grown
Fairer with time, and tenderer in its tone,
As when in August woods a second burst
Of leaves is seen more golden than the first.
A woman truly to be loved—but loving ?
There was the riddle wit despaired of proving,

For who can read the stars ?   I sat with her
The evening through, and rose up happier :
In all that crowd there was no single face
Worthy her notice, not to say her grace,
And once again her charm was on my soul.
" If she love any "—this was still the goal
Of my night thoughts in argument with fear—
" Say what they will, the lover is not here."
Not here !   And yet, at parting, she had pressed
Manton's sole hand, and nodded to the rest.

Four days I lived in my fool's paradise,
Importuning Griselda's changing eyes
With idle flattery.   I found her mood
Softer than once in her young womanhood,
Yet restless and uncertain.   There were hours
Of a wild gaiety, when all the powers
Of her keen mind were in revolt with folly,
Others bedimmed with wordless melancholy.
Once too or twice she shocked me with a phrase
Of doubtful sense, revealing thoughts and ways

New to her past, an echo of the noise
Of that mad world we lived in and its joys :
Such things were sacrilege.   I could not see
Unmoved my angel smirched with vanity,
Even though, it seemed at moments, for my sake.
Her laughter, when she laughed, made my heart
    ache,
And I had spared some pain to see her sad
Rather than thus unseasonably glad.

Who would have dreamed it ?   Each new idle
    day,
When, tired with sport, we rested from the fray,
Five jovial shooters, jaded by the sun,
Seeking refreshment at the stroke of noon,—
There, with the luncheon carts all trimly dight,
Stood Lady L., to the fool crowd's delight.
You would have thought her life had always been
Passed in the stubbles, as, with questions keen,
She eyed the bags and parleyed with the "guns ; "
Rome's matron she with us the Goths and Huns.

Young Manton proudly spread for her his coat

Under a hedge, and she resented not.

Resented ! Why resent ? Nay, smiles were there.

And a swift look of pleasure, still more rare,

Pleasure and gratitude, as though the act

Had been of chivalry in form and fact

Transcending Raleigh's. Ay, indeed ! Resent !

That eye were blind which doubted what it meant.

And still I doubted. Vanity dies hard.

And love, however starving of reward,

And youth's creed of belief. It seemed a thing

Monstrous, impossible, bewildering,

As tales of dwarfs and giants gravely told

By men of science, and transmuted gold,

And magic potions turning men to beasts,

And lewd witch Sabbaths danced by unfrocked
　　priests.

Griselda ! Manton ! In what mood or tense

Could folly conjugate such dreams to sense,

Or draw the contract not in terms absurd

Of such a friendship or of act or word ?

Where was the common thought between the
  two—

Even of partridges—the other knew ?

Manton—Griselda !   Nay 'twere fabulous,

A mere profanity, to argue thus ;

Only I watched them closer when they strayed

To gather blackberries, as boy and maid

In a first courting, and her eager eyes

Turned as he spoke, and laughter came unwise

Before she answered, and an hour was flown,

Before he joined the rest and she was gone.

  O Love ! what an absurdity thou art,

How heedless of proportion, whole or part !

Time, place, occasion, what are they to thee ?

Thou playest the wanton with Solemnity,

The prince with Poverty, the rogue with Worth,

The fool with all the Wisdoms of the Earth.

Thou art a leveller, more renowned than Death,

For he, when in his rage he stops our breath,

Leaves us at least the harvest of our years,

The right to be heroic in our tears.

But thou dost only mock.   Thou art a king

Dealing with slaves, who waits no questioning,

But gives—to this a province and a crown,

To that a beggar's staff and spangled gown ;

And when some weep their undeserved disgrace,

Plucks at their cheeks and smites them in the face.

Thou hast no reverence, no respect for right.

Virtue to thee is a lewd appetite,

Remorse a pastime, modesty a lure,

And love, the malady, love's only cure.

Griselda, in her love at thirty-three,

Was the supreme fool of felicity.

Reason and she had taken separate roads,

A spectacle of mirth for men and gods.

And the world laughed—discreetly in its sleeves—

At her poor artless shifts and make-believes.

For it was true, true to the very text,

This whispered thing that had my soul perplexed,

Manton was her beloved—by what art,

What mute equation of the human heart,

What blind jibe of dame Fortune, who shall say?

The road of passion is no king's highway,

Mapped out with finger-posts for all to see,

But each soul journeys on it separately,

And only those who have walked its mazes through

Remember on what paths the wild flowers grew.

Ay, who shall say? Nor had the truth been sung,

Save for the incontinence of Manton's tongue,

Wagging in argument on certain themes,

With boast of craft in pleasure's stratagems.

"For Love" ('twas thus he made his parable

In cynic phrase, as hero of his tale,

One evening when the others were abed,

And we two sat on smoking, head to head,

Discoursing in that tone of men scarce friends,

Who prate philosophy to candle ends),

"Love, though its laws have not as yet been written

By any Balzac for our modern Britain,

And though perhaps there is no strategy
Youth can quite count upon or argue by,
Is none the less an art, with some few rules
Wise men observe, who would outrun the fools.
Now, for myself" (here Manton spread his hands
With professorial wave in white wrist-bands)
"I hold it as a maxim always wise
In making love to deal with contraries.
Colours, books tell us, to be strongly blent,
Need opposite colours for their complement,
And so too women whose ill-reasoning mind
Requires some contradiction to be kind."

"It is not enough in this late year of grace
To answer fools with their own foolishness—
Rather with your best wisdom.   You will need
Your folly to perplex some wiser head.
And so my maxim is, whatever least
Women expect, that thing will serve you best.
Thus, with young souls in their first unfledged years,
Ask their opinion as philosophers :

Consult their knowledge in the ways of life.

The repute of sin will please a too chaste wife.

Your deference keep for harlots: these you
   touch

Best by your modesty, which makes them blush.

With a proud beauty deal out insolence,

And bear her fence down with a stronger fence.

She will be angry, but a softer cheek

Turn to the smiter who has proved her weak.

And so with wisdom : meet it with surprise,

Laugh at it idly gazing in its eyes,

Leave it no solid ground for its fair feet,

And lead it lightly where love's waters meet.

Even virtue—virtue of the noblest type,

The fair sad woman, whose romance is ripe,

Needs but a little knowledge to be led,

Perhaps less than the rest if truth be said.

You must not parley with her.   Words are vain,

And you might wake some half forgotten pain.

Avoid her soul.   It is a place too strong

For your assaulting, and a siege were long.

Others have failed before it. Touch it not,
But march beyond, nor fire a single shot.
The fields of pleasure less defended lie :
These are your vantage-ground for victory.
Strike boldly for possession and command ;
An hour may win it, if you hold her hand.
I knew one once : " . . .

           I would have stopped him here
But for the shame which held me prisoner ;
And his undaunted reassuring smile,
Commanding confidence. "I knew once on a
    while,"
He said, "a woman whom the world called
    proud,
A saintly soul, untouched by the vain crowd,
Who had survived all battle, siege, and sack,
Love ever led with armies at his back,
Yet fell at last to the mere accident
Of a chance meeting, for another meant :
Her lover had not dared it, had he known,

But faces in the dark are all as one.
You know the rhyme."

                 But at this point I rose,
Fearing what worse his folly might disclose,
And having learned my lesson of romance,
A sadder man and wiser for the chance,
Bade him good night: (it was in truth good-
    bye,
For pretexting next morning some small lie
Of business calling me in haste to town,
I fled the house). He looked me up and
    down,
Yawned, rose to light his candle at the lamp,
Pressed with warm hand my own hand which was
    damp,
And as he sauntered cheerily to bed,
I heard him sing—they linger in my head—
The first staves of a ballad, then the fashion
With the young bloods who shape their love and
    passion

At the music-halls of the Metropolis;
What I remember of the song was this :

  But, no, I cannot write it.   There are things
Too bitter in their taste, and this one stings
My soul to a mad anger even yet.
I seem to hear the voices of the pit
Lewdly discoursing of incestuous scenes,
  Bottom the weaver's and the enamoured queen's.
Alas, Titania ! thou poor soul, alas !
How art thou fallen, and to what an ass !

CHAPTER V.

GRISELDA's madness lasted forty days,
Forty eternities !   Men went their ways,
And suns arose and set, and women smiled,
And tongues wagged lightly in impeachment wild
Of Lady L.'s adventure.   She was gone,
None knew by whom escorted or alone,
Or why or whither, only that one morning,
Without pretext or subterfuge or warning,
She had disappeared in silence from L. House,
Leaving her lord in multitudinous
And agonised conjecture of her fate :
So the tale went.   And truly less sedate
Than his wont was in intricate affairs,
Such as his Garter or his lack of heirs,

Lord L. was seen in this new tribulation.

Griselda long had been his life's equation,

The pivot of his dealings with the world,

The mainstay of his comfort, all now hurled

To unforeseen confusion by her flight :

There was need of action swift and definite.

Where was she? Who could tell him? Divers
   visions

Passed through his fancy—thieves, and street
   collisions,

And all the hundred accidents of towns,

From broken axle trees to broken crowns.

In vain he questioned ; no response was made

More than the fact that, as already said,

My lady, unattended and on foot,

(A sad imprudence here Lord L. took note),

Had gone out dressed in a black morning gown

And dark tweed waterproof, 'twixt twelve and one,

Leaving no orders to her maid, or plan

About her carriage to or groom or man.

Such was in sum the downstairs' evidence.

The hall porter, a man of ponderous sense,

Averred her ladyship had eastward turned

From the front door, and some small credit

    earned

For the suggestion that her steps were bent

To Whitechapel on merciful intent,

A visit of compassion to the poor,

A clue which led to a commissioner

Being sent for in hot haste from Scotland Yard.

And so the news was bruited abroad.

    It reached my ears among the earliest,

And from Lord L. himself, whose long suppressed

Emotion found its vent one afternoon

On me, the only listener left in town.

His thoughts now ran on "a religious craze

Of his poor wife's," he said, "in these last days

Indulged beyond all reason." The police

Would listen to no talk of casualties,

Still less of crime, since they had nothing found

In evidence above or under ground,

                 G

But held the case to be of simpler kind,
Home left in a disordered state of mind
Lord L. had noticed, now they talked of it,
Temper less equable and flightier wit,
"A craving for religious services
And sacred music." Something was amiss,
Or why were they in London in September?
Griselda latterly, he could remember,
Had raved of a conventual retreat
In terms no Protestant would deem discreet,
As the sole refuge in a world of sin
For human frailty, grief's best anodyne.
"The *Times* was right. Rome threatened to absorb us :
    absorb us :
The convents must be searched by *habeas corpus.*"

And so I came to help him. I had guessed
From his first word the vainness of his quest,
And half was moved to serve him in a strait
Where her fair fame I loved was in debate,
Yet held my peace, nor hazarded a word

Save of surprise at the strange case I heard,

Till, fortune aiding, I should find the clue

My heart desired to do what I would do.

And not in vain.   Night found me duly sped, ;

Lord L.'s ambassador accredited,

With fullest powers to find and fetch her home,

If need should be, from the Pope's jaws in Rome.

Gods ! what a mission ! First my round I went

Through half the slums of Middlesex and Kent,

Surrey and Essex—this to soothe Lord L.,

Though witless all, as my heart told too well ;

The hospitals no less and casual wards,

Each house as idly as his House of Lords,

And only at the week's end dared to stop

At the one door I knew still housing hope,

Young Manton's chambers.   There, with reddened
  cheek

I heard the answer given I came to seek :

Manton was gone, his landlady half feared

He too, in some mishap, and disappeared,—

Proof all too positive.   His letters lay
A fortnight deep untouched upon the tray.
She could not forward them or risk a guess
As to his last or likeliest address.
He was in Scotland often at this season,
"But not without his guns"—a cogent reason,
And leaving, too, his valet here in town,
Perplexed of what to do or leave undone.
Abroad ?   Perhaps.   If so, his friends might try
As a best chance the Paris Embassy.
He had been there last Spring, and might be now.

Paris !   It was enough, I made my bow,
And took my leave.   I seemed to touch the thread
Of the blind labyrinth 'twas mine to tread.
Where should they be, in truth, these too fond
    lovers,
But in the land of all such lawless rovers :
The land of Gautier, Bourget, Maupassant,
Where still "you can" makes answer to "I can't :"
The fair domain where all romance begins

In a light borderland of venial sins,

But deepening onwards, till the fatal day

Vice swoops upon us, plead we as we may.

Griselda's bonnet o'er the windmills thrown,

Had surely crossed the Seine e'er it came down;

And I, if I would find and win her back,

Must earliest search the boulevards for her
    track :

And so to Paris in my zeal I passed,

Breaking my idol, mad Iconoclast.

There is a little inn by Meudon wood

Dear to Parisians in their amorous mood,

A place of rendezvous, where bourgeois meet

Their best beloved in congregation sweet :

Clandestine, undisturbed, illicit loves,

Made half romantic by the adjoining groves,

So beautiful in spring, with the new green

Clothing the birch stems scattered white between,

Nor yet, in autumn, when the first frosts burn,

And the wind rustles in the reddening fern,

Quite robbed of sentiment for lovers' eyes,

Who seek earth's blessing on a bliss unwise,

And find the happy sanction for their state

In nature's face, unshocked by their debate,

As who should say " Let preachers frown their fill,

Here one approves.   'Tis Eden with us still."

Such fancy, may be, in her too fond heart

Had led Griselda—with her friend—apart,

Yet not apart, from the world's curious gaze,

To this secluded, ill-frequented place :

A compromise of wills and varying moods,

His for gay crowds, her own for solitudes.

Manton knew Paris well, and loved its noise,

Its mirthful parody of serious joys,

Its pomp and circumstance.   His wish had been

To flaunt the boulevards with his captured queen,

And make parade of a last triumph won

In the chaste field of prudish Albion,

Outscandalising scandal.   Love and he

In any sense but of male vanity,

And the delirium of adventures new

In the world's eye—the thing he next should do—

Were terms diverse and incompatible.

Griselda, to his eyes, was Lady L.,

The fair, the chaste, the unapproached proud
  name

Men breathed in reverence, woman, all the same,

And not as such, and when the truth was said,

Worth more than others lightlier credited.

It all had been a jest from the beginning,

A *tour de force*, whose wit was in the winning,

A stroke of fortune and of accident,

The embrace he had told of for another meant,

While she stood grieving for a first grey hair

(A psychologic moment) on the stair,

And, kneeling down, he had adored her foot,

The one weak spot where her self-love had root,

And laughed at her, and told her she was old,

Yet growing tenderer as he grew more bold ;

And so from jest to jest, and chance to chance,

To that last scene at the mad country dance

Where she had played the hoyden, he the swain,

Pretending love till love was in their brain,

And he had followed to her chamber door,

And helped her to undo the dress she wore.

Then the elopement.   That had been her doing,

Which he accepted to make good his wooing,

And careless what to both the result might be,

So it but served his end of vanity.

It all had been to this vain boy a whim,

Something grotesque, a play, a pantomime,

Where nothing had been serious but her heart,

And that was soon too tearful for its part.

He wearied in a week of her mature

Old maidish venturings in ways obscure,

Her agony of conscience dimly guessed,

The silences she stifled in her breast,

Her awkwardness—it was his word—in all

That love could teach ; her sighs funereal,

And more the unnatural laughter she essayed

To meet the doubtful sense of things he said.

She **was** at once too tender and too prim,

Too prudish and too crazed with love and him.

At a month's end his flame had leaped beyond

Already to friends frailer and less fond,

The light Parisian world of venal charms

Which welcomed him with wide and laughing

    arms :

There he was happier, more at home, more gay,

King of the "high life," hero of the day.

    Griselda, in her sad suburban nook

Watched his departures with a mute rebuke,

Yet daring not to speak.   The choice was hers

To stay at home or run the theatres

With her young lover in such company

As her soul loathed.   She had tried despairingly

To be one, even as these, for his loved sake,

And would have followed spite of her heart's ache,

But that he hardly further cared to press,

After one failure, stamped with " dowdiness : "

That too had been his word, a bitter word,

Biting and true, which smote her like a sword,
Or rather a whip's sting to her proud cheek,
Leaving her humbled, agonised and weak.

Poor beautiful Griselda !   What was now
The value of thy beauty, chaste as snow
In thy youth's morning, the unchallenged worth
Of thy eyes' kindness, queenliest of the earth ;
The tradition of thy Fra-angelic face,
Blessed as Mary's, and as full of grace ;
The fame which thou despisedst, yet which made
A glory for thee meet for thy dear head ?
What, if in this last crisis of thy fate,
When all a heaven and hell was in debate,
And thy archangel, with the feet of clay,
Stood mocking there in doubt to go or stay,
The unstable fabric of thy woman's dower,
Thy beauty, failed and left thee in *their* power
Whose only law of beauty was the sting
Lent to man's lust by light bedizening ?
What use was in thy beauty, if, alas !

Thou gavest them cause to mock—those tongues
of brass—
At thy too crude and insular attire,
Thy naïvetés of colour, the false fire
Of thy first dallyings with the red and white,
Thy sweet pictorial robes, Pre-Raphaelite,
Quaint in their tones and *outrées* in design,
Thy lack of unity and shape and line,
Thy English angularity—who knows,
The less than perfect fitting of thy shoes?

Griselda, in her flight, had left behind
All but the dress she stood in, too refined,
In her fair righteousness of thought and deed,
To make provision for a future need,
However dire.   She was no Israelite
To go forth from her Pharaoh in the night,
With spoils of the Egyptians in her hands,
And had thrown herself on Manton and on France
With a full courage worth a nobler cause,
Grandly oblivious of prudential laws.

Her earliest trouble, marring even the bliss
Of love's first ecstasy, had come of this,
Her want of clothes—a worse and weightier care
At the mere moment than her soul's despair
For its deep fall from virtuous estate.
How should she dress herself, she asked of Fate,
With neither maid, nor money, nor a name?
It was her first experiment in shame.
Now, after all her poor economies,
This was the ending read in his vexed eyes,
And spoken by his lips : her utmost art
Had failed to please that idle thing, his heart,
Or even to avert his petulant scorn
For one so little to love's manner born.

And thus I found them, at the angry noon
Of their "red month," the next to honeymoon :
Two silent revellers at a loveless feast,
Scared by hate's morning breaking in their east—
A dawn which was of penance and despair,
With pleasure's ghost to fill the vacant chair.

I took it, and was welcomed rapturously,

As a far sail by shipwrecked souls at sea,

An opportune deliverer, timely sent

To break the autumn of their discontent,

And give a pretext to their need grown sore

Of issue from joys dead by any door.

Manton, all confidential from the first,

Told me the tale of his last sins and worst,

As meriting a sympathy not less

Than the best actions virtuous men confess.

He was overwhelmed with women and with
    debt—

Women who loved him, bills which must be met.

What could he do? Her ladyship was mad—

It was her fault, not his, this escapade.

He had warned her from the first, and as a
    friend,

That all such frolics had a serious end,

And that to leave her home was the worst way

A woman would who wanted to be gay.

"For look," said he, "we men, who note these
　　things,
And how the unthinking flutterers burn their wings,
Know that a woman, be she what she will,
The fairest, noblest, most adorable,
Dowered in her home with all seraphic charms,
Whom heaven itself might envy in your arms,
A paragon of pleasure undenied
At her own chaste respectable fireside,
Becomes, what shall I say, when she steps down
From the high world of her untouched renown—
A something differing in no serious mood
From the sad rest of the light sisterhood:
Perhaps indeed more troublesome than these,
Because she keenlier feels the agonies :
A wounded soul, who has not even the wit
To hide its hurt and make a jest of it;
A maid of Astolat, launched in her barge,
A corpse on all the world, a *femme à charge.*"

"'Tis not," he argued, " our poor human sins

That make us what we are when shame begins,

But the world pointing at our naked state :

Then we are shocked and humbled at our fate,

Silent and shamed in all we honour most—

For what is virtue but the right to boast ?

A married woman's love, three weeks from home,

Is the absurdest thing in Christendom,

Dull as a *ménage* in the demi-monde

And dismaller far by reason of the bond.

All this I told my lady ere we went,

But warning wasted is on sentiment.

You see the net result here in one word,

A crying woman and a lover bored."

So far young Manton.   She for whom I came,

Griselda's self, sweet soul, in her new shame

Essayed awhile to hide from me the truth

Of this last hap of her belated youth,

Her disillusion with her graceless lover.

She made sad cloaks for him which could not

cover

His great unworthiness and her despair,
All with a frightened half-maternal air,
Most pitiful and touching.   To my plea,
Urging her home, she answered mournfully,
That she was bound now to her way of life,
And owed herself no less than as his wife
To him she had chosen out of all mankind.
'Twas better to be foolish, even blind,
If he had faults, so she could serve him still—
And this had been her promise and her will.
She would not hear of duties owed elsewhere :
What was she to Lord L., or he to her ?
I need not speak of it.   And yet she clung
To my protecting presence in her wrong ;
And once, when Manton's jibes made bitterer play,
Implored me with appealing eyes to stay.
And so I lingered on.

              Those autumn days,
Spent with Griselda in the woodland ways
Of Meudon with her lover, or alone,

When his mad fancies carried him to town,

Remain to me an unsubstantial act

Of dreaming fancy, rather than the fact

Of any waking moment in my past,

The sweetest, saddest, and with her the last—

For suddenly they ended.

                    We had been

One Sunday for a jaunt upon the Seine,

We two—in Manton's absence, now prolonged

To a third night—and in a steamboat, thronged

With idle bourgeois folk, whom the last glory

Of a late autumn had sent forth in foray

To Passy and St. Cloud, from stage to stage,

Had made with heavy souls our pilgrimage ;

And homeward turning and with little zest,

The fair day done, to love's deserted nest

Had come with lagging feet and weary eyes,

Expectant still of some new dark surprise,

When the blow fell unsparing on her head,

Already by what fortunes buffeted.

                                        H

How did it happen, that last tragedy ?—

For tragedy it was, let none deny,

Though all ignoble.   Every soul of us

Touches one moment in death's darkened house

The plane of the heroic, and compels

Men's laughter into tears—ay, heaven's and hell's.

How did it happen?   There was that upon

Their faces at the door more than the tone

Of their replies, that warned us of the thing

We had not looked for in our questioning ;

And our lips faltered, and our ears, afraid,

Shrank from more hearing.   What was it they said

In their fool's jargon, that he lay upstairs ?

He ?   Manton ?   The dispenser of our cares ?

The mountebank young reveller ? Suffering ?   Ill ?

And she, poor soul, that suffered at his will !

A sinister case ?   Not dying ?   Pitiful God !

Truly Thou smitest blindly with Thy rod.

For Manton was not worthy to die young,

Beloved by her with blessings on her tongue.

And such a cause of death !

She never heard

The whole truth told, for each one spared his word,

And he lay mute for ever.   But to me

The thing was storied void of mystery,

And thus they told it.   Hardly had we gone

On our sad river outing, when from town

Manton had come with a gay troop of friends,

Such as the *coulisse* of the opera lends,

To breakfast at the inn and spend the day

In mirthful noise, as was his vagrant way.

A drunken frolic, and most insolent

To her whose honour with his own was blent,

To end in this last tragedy.   None knew

Quite how it happened, or a cause could shew

Further than this, that, rising from the table

The last to go, with steps perhaps unstable—

For they had feasted freely, and the stair

Was steep and iron-edged, and needed care ;

And singing, as he went, the selfsame song,

Which I remembered, to the laughing throng,

He had slipped his length, and fallen feet-first down.

When they picked him up his power to move was
    gone,
Though he could speak.   They laid him on a bed,
Her bed, Griselda's, and called in with speed
Such help of doctors and commissioners
As law prescribed, and medicine for their fears.
'Twas his last night.

             There, in Griselda's hands,
Young Jerry Manton lay with the last sands
Of his life's hour-glass trickling to its close,
Griselda watching, with what thoughts, God
    knows.
We did not speak.   But her lips moved in prayer,
And mine too, in the way of man's despair.
I did not love him, yet a human pity
Softened my eyes.   Afar, from the great city,
The sound came to us of the eternal hum,
Unceasing, changeless, pregnant with all doom
Of insolent life that rises from its streets,
The pulse of sin which ever beats and beats,

Wearying the ears of God.   O Paris, Paris !

What doom is thine for every soul that tarries

Too long with thee, a stranger in thy arms.

Thy smiles are incantations, thy brave charms

Death to thy lovers.   Each gay mother's son,

Smitten with love for thee, is straight undone.

And lo the chariot wheels upon thy ways !

And a new garland hung in *Père la Chaise !*

Poor soul !   I turned and looked into the night,

Through the uncurtained windows, and there bright

Saw the mute twinkle of a thousand stars.

One night ! the least in all time's calendars,

Yet fraught with what a meaning for this one !

One star, the least of all that million !

One room in that one city !   Yet for him

The universe there was of space and time.

What were his thoughts ?   In that chaotic soul,

Home of sad jests, obscene, unbeautiful,

Mired with the earthiest of brute desires,

And lit to sentience only with lewd fires,

Was there no secret, undisturbed, fair place
Watered with love and favoured with God's grace
To which the wounded consciousness had fled
For its last refuge from a world of dread?
Was his soul touched to tenderness, to awe,
To softer recollection?   All we saw
Was the maimed body gasping forth its breath,
A rigid setting of the silent teeth,
And the hands trembling.   Death was with us
    there.
But where was he—O Heaven of pity! where?

We watched till morning by the dying man,
She weeping silently, I grieved and wan,
And still he moved not.   But with the first break
Of day in the window panes we saw him make
A sign as if of speaking.   Pressing near—
For his lips moved, Griselda deemed, in prayer—
We heard him make profession of his faith,
As a man of pleasure face to face with death,
A kind of gambler's Athanasian Creed,

Repeated at the hour of his last need.

" Five sovereigns," said he, steadying his will,

As in defiance of death's power to kill,

And with that smile of a superior mind,

Which was his strength in dealing with mankind,

The world of sporting jargon and gay livers.

" Five sovereigns is a fiver, and five fivers

A pony, and five ponies are a hundred—

No, four," he added, seeing he had blundered.

" *Four* to the hundred and *five* centuries

Make up the monkey." From his dying eyes

The smile of triumph faded. " There, I've done it,"

He said, " but there was no great odds upon it,

You see with a broken back."

                      He spoke no more,

And in another hour had passed the door

Which shuts the living from eternity.

Where was he? God of pity, where was he?

This was the end of Lady L.'s romance.

When we had buried him, as they do in
    France,
In a tomb inscribed " *à perpétuité* "
(Formally rented till the Judgment Day),
She put off black, and shed no further tears ;
Her face for the first time showed all its years,
But not a trace beyond. Without demur
She gave adhesion to my plans for her,
And we went home to London and Lord L.,
Silent together, by the next night's mail.
She had been six weeks away.

               The interview
Between them was dramatic. I, who knew
Her whole mad secret, and had seen her soul
Stripped of its covering, and without control,
Bowed down by circumstance and galled with
    shame,
Yielding to wounds and griefs without a name,
Had feared for her a wild unhappy scene.
I held Lord L. for the least stern of men,

And yet I dared not hope even he would crave
No explanation e'er he quite forgave.

    I was with them when they met, unwilling
       third,
In their mute bandying of the unspoken word.
Lord L. essayed to speak. I saw his face
Made up for a high act of tragic grace
As he came forward. It was grave and mild,
A father's welcoming a truant child,
Forgiving, yet intent to mark the pain
With hope "the thing should not occur again."
His lips began to move as to some speech
Framed in this sense, as one might gently
      preach
A word in season to too gadding wives
Of duties owed, at least by those whose lives
Moved in high places. But it died unsaid.
There was that about Griselda that forbade
Marital questionings. Her queenly eyes
Met his with a mute answer of surprise,

Marking the unseemliness of all display

More strongly than with words, as who should
    say

Noblesse oblige.   She took his outstretched hand,

And kissed his cheek, but would not under-
    stand

A word of his reproaches.   Even I,

With my full knowledge and no more a boy,

But versed by years in the world's wickedness,

And open-eyed to her, alas ! no less

Than to all womanhood, even I felt shame,

And half absolved her in my mind from blame.

And he, how could he less?   He was but
    human,

The fortunate husband of how fair a woman !

He stammered his excuses.

                        What she told

When I had left them (since all coin is gold

To those who would believe, and who the key

Hold of their eyes, in blind faith's alchemy)

I never learned.

I did not linger on,

Seeing her peril past and the day won,

But took my leave.   She led me to the door

With her old kindness of the days of yore,

And thanked me as one thanks for little things.

" You have been," she said, "an angel without
  wings,

And I shall not forget,—nor will Lord L. ;

And yet," she said, with an imperceptible

Change in her voice, "there are things the world
  will say

Which are neither just nor kind, and, if to-day

We part awhile, remember we are friends,

If not now later.   Time will make amends,

And we shall meet again."   I pressed her hand

A moment to my lips.   " I understand,"

I said, and gazed a last time in her eyes ;

" Say all you will.   I am your sacrifice."

And so, in truth, it was.   Henceforth there lay

A gulf between us, widening with delay,

And which our souls were impotent to pass,

The gulf of a dead secret ; and, alas !

Who knows what subtle treacheries within,

For virtue rends its witnesses of sin,

And hearts are strangely fashioned by their fears.

We met no more in friendship through the
     years,

Although I held her secret as my own,

And fought her battles, her best champion,

On many a stricken field in scandal's war,

Till all was well forgotten.   From afar

I watched her fortunes still with tenderness,

Yet sadly, as cast out of Paradise.

For ever, spite her promise, from that day,

When I met L., he looked another way ;

And she, Griselda, was reserved and chill.

I had behaved, her women friends said, ill,

And caused a needless scandal in her life,

—They told not what.   Enough, that as a wife

She had been compelled to close her doors on me,

And that her lord knew all the iniquity.

And so I bore the burden of her sin.

What more shall I relate?   The cynic vein
Has overwhelmed my tale, and I must stop.
Its heroine lived to justify all hope
Of her long-suffering lord, that out of pain
Blessings would grow, and his house smile again
With the fulfilled expectance of an heir.
Griselda sat no longer in despair,
Nor wasted her full life on dreams of folly ;
She had little time for moods of melancholy,
Or heart to venture further in love's ways ;
She was again the theme of all men's praise,
And suffered no man's passion.   Once a year,
In the late autumn, when the leaves grew sere
She made retreat to a lay sisterhood,
And lived awhile there for her soul's more good,
In pious meditation, fasts and prayer.
Some say she wore concealed a shirt of hair
Under her dresses, even at court balls,
And certain 'tis that all Rome's rituals

Were followed daily at the private Mass

In her new chauntry built behind Hans Place.

Lord L. approved of all she did, even this,

Strange as it seemed to his old fashionedness.

He, gentle soul, grown garrulous with years,

Prosed of her virtues to all listeners,

And of their son's, the child of his old age,

A prodigy of beauty and ways sage.

It was a vow, he said, once made in Rome,

Had brought them this chief treasure of their
home.

A vow ! The light world laughed—for miracles

Are not believed in now, except as hell's.

And yet the ways of God are passing strange.

And this is certain (and therein the range

Of my long tale is reached, and I am free),

—There is at Ostia, close beside the sea,

A convent church, the same where years ago

Griselda kneeled in tears and made her vow ;

And in that shrine, beneath the crucifix,

They show a votive offering, candlesticks
Of more than common workmanship and size,
And underneath inscribed the votary's
Name in initials, and the date, all told,
Hall-marked in England, and of massive gold.

THE END.

Printed by BALLANTYNE, HANSON & CO.
Edinburgh and London

www.ingramcontent.com/pod-product-compliance
Lightning Source LLC
Chambersburg PA
CBHW020412030726
47496CB00007B/2420